A GOOSEBUMPS
STORY

DOG'S JOURNEY

A GOOSEY FARM STORY

DOG'S JOURNEY

GENE KEMP

Illustrated by Paul Howard

CollinsChildren'sBooks

An imprint of HarperCollins*Publishers*

First published in Great Britain by
CollinsChildren'sBooks1996

1 3 5 7 9 8 6 4 2
CollinsChildren'sBooks is a division of
HarperCollins Publishers Ltd.,
77-85 Fulham Palace Road,
Hammersmith, London W6 8JB

Text copyright © Gene Kemp 1996
Illustrations copyright © Paul Howard 1996

The author and illustrator assert the moral right to be
identified as the author and illustrator of the work.

Printed and bound in Great Britain
by Caledonian International Book Manufacturing Ltd.,
Glasgow G64

ISBN HB 0 00 185630 8
ISBN PB 0 00 675137 7

For Ann-Janine –
and for Jenny,
the dog who chased hens.

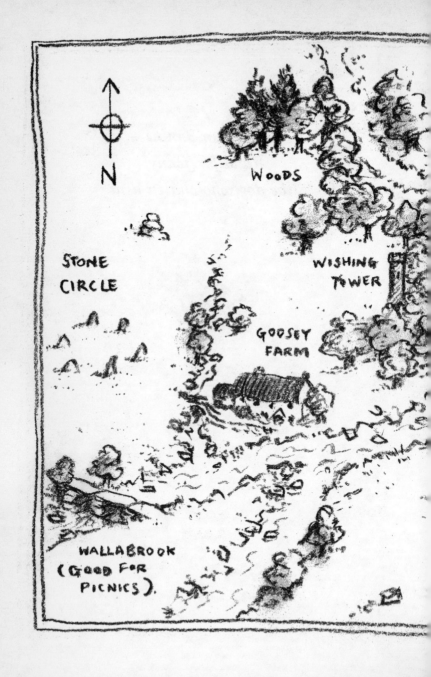

N

WOODS

STONE
CIRCLE

WISHING
TOWER

GOOSEY
FARM

WALLABROOK
(GOOD FOR
PICNICS).

ANCIENT
BURIAL
CHAMBER

TO SCHOOL

STONEY
FARM

RIVER
TEIGN

TO
TOWN

MAIN
ROAD

Chapter One

PICTURE A DEVON VALLEY

Once at night we watched young badgers play in the moonlight, running and racing, twisting and turning, frisking and gambolling among the trees. Their striped coats shone silver in the moonbeams sliding down between the pale tree trunks where their mother watched, keeping guard over them. We held our dogs, Russet and Dizzy Frizzy, quivering on their leads until the badgers melted away into the dark as suddenly and as silently as they'd appeared in the clearing of the wood near where we lived.

And once as we walked over Hunter's Path, high above the river rushing through the narrow gorge more than a hundred feet below, a red deer leapt out of the heather on to the path, then jumped round to face Russet, whose own coat was as red as that of the deer. They stared at each other – for ever, it seemed – while we stood like statues, even little Dizzy Frizzy. At last Russet barked and away bounded the deer over the rocks and the bracken, with Russet just behind running like the wind.

But even she couldn't catch the deer. Whatever would we have done if she had?

When Russet came back to us, ears up, eyes shining, tail wagging, body waggling, Dizzy Frizzy sniffed and licked her furiously to find out just what she'd been up to. Russet pushed her away, then lifted her nose in the air and led the way triumphantly, the Leader, the Boss, Top Dog Russet.

Picture a Devon valley, hills all around, the purple moor rising behind them, a tumbling rocky stream with little rowan trees and an ancient stone-and-cob farmhouse. It was called Goosey Farm and it was old when Queen Elizabeth the First sent the laughing pirate, Sir Francis Drake, to fight the Spanish Armada sailing up the Channel to conquer England. He said they must wait till he'd finished playing bowls on Plymouth Hoe. Then he sent them far away as fast as they could go. The beacons on Dartmoor and Exmoor were lit but Devon (and Goosey Farm) were safe from Spaniards. Mind you,

it had already survived the Normans – William the Conqueror named it in his Domesday Book – and before them, the Saxons and the Romans.

We'd come from a little terraced house in a city to Goosey Farm with its two staircases and rooms that went on for ever and ever so you could never finish exploring. There were beams in the ceilings and panelling on the walls and a fireplace as wide as a gate with a wooden seat built into it.

Tiny windows sat in walls as wide as your outstretched arms, while the back of the house crouched under a steep hill that sheltered Goosey from the winds and the

winter snows. In the city we'd only had a concrete yard with a bush, but now we had a wild sloping garden full of crooked fruit trees with strange names like medlar and quince and covered in furry mossy stuff called lichen – and beyond the garden lay the fields and the moor.

Raggedy rugs were scattered on the stone floors and old wooden chairs stood around like people. When we found the two staircases I chased Tim and the dogs round and round and round and then round and round and round the other way until Mum yelled,

"Stop! You're driving me crazy!"

My bedroom had a ceiling bulging nearly down to my head and we put books under one leg of the bed to keep it level.

There was a secret door in the corner and honeysuckle and roses tried to climb over the window-sill away from the broken drainpipe outside.

"Mending that drainpipe's the first job," Dad said when he saw it. "Your mother'll enjoy doing that," and ducked as she threw something at him. My dad's a joker but Mum stands up to him. He's in the Navy and goes away a lot but comes back with presents for us that he calls "rabbits": funny things, old books, carved wooden animals and clockwork toys that only work sometimes.

In my room were tons of books and my collection of teddies and woolly animals and a farm. At night Russet and Dizzy Frizzy slept under the patchwork quilt on my bed. They creep up when it gets dark. They're not supposed to. I don't know if Mum knows. If anyone comes we all lie dead still.

Tim's room's quite far away, round a corner and down a passage. He's got hundreds of models: ships, aeroplanes everywhere and hanging from the ceiling so you bump into them if you're not careful. And he's got two gerbils in cages. Old Harry the hamster is in my room and I have to get him out to check that he's still alive as he's really old now, for a hamster, that is. I don't want him to die. But I know he will some day. Not yet though. Not yet.

At night I tell Russet and Dizzy Frizzy all about everything, especially Russet. She's got ears that spring up and down as I talk. Russet's my best friend – especially now we've moved and I've left my school pals behind.

"You'll soon make new ones," Mum told me. "Honest."

When Russet gets tired of me talking she puts her tail down, turns round twice, pushes her nose under the patchwork quilt and follows it till she's covered, thumps herself down with a heavy sigh, curls up and goes to sleep on top of my feet usually, so I can't move. Dizzy Frizzy then copies her. Dizzy Frizzy always does what Russet does. If she can.

Someone eventually turned up to mend that drainpipe. He stood on a ladder under my bedroom window.

"What's your name?" I asked.

"Fred," he answered, tapping the drainpipe with a hammer.

"Fred what?" I asked.

"Just Fred."

"OK, I'll call you Just Fred."

"You're quick. What's your name?"

"The Widget."

"That's a funny name," said Fred.

"It's 'cos I'm little and wriggle into small spaces. Are you a gypsy?" I asked, for Fred wore a red scarf round his neck and a gold earring in one ear. His hair was tied back in a ponytail.

"No, but I'd like to be. I'd like to ride round the world on my motorbike and not have to work every day mending pipes and drains."

Dinah came and leant out of the window beside me so that her hair fell down over the drainpipe and the honeysuckle. Dinah is Dad's sister and my aunt and her hair is black and her eyes are green.

"Ouch," yelled Fred, hitting his thumb with the hammer which dropped down among the nettles growing over the drain at the bottom.

"I don't know who you are," he called to Dinah, "but will you come round the world with me on my motorbike?"

"No," she answered, shut the window with a bang and walked out of the room. I opened the window again slowly, not very far.

"She's all right really," I told him.

"I can see that." He grinned at me. "Wow."

★

That walk where we saw the deer on Hunter's Path was our first *real* walk with Dad, Mum, Tim, Dinah and me. Right at the start of our trail, with just his tail showing as we walked through the bracken, the heather and the tufty grass came Sam Cat, our big tom cat and the only one of our animals who could put Russet down. He did this by scratching her tender nose. For Sam too was a Boss. All the farm cats – don't mention the rats or mice! – kept away from Sam. You could imagine little notices on the cob walls –

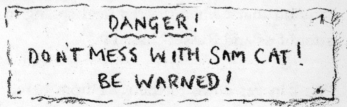

He came on our walk 'cos he couldn't bear to be left behind.

We'd only just set out when suddenly Fred appeared wearing an enormous plaid jacket. I was pleased.

"Thought you might get lost so I joined you," he grinned.

"I thought you worked all the time," I said.

"Never on Sundays."

Dinah sniffed and moved up to walk with Mum.

After a bit, Dad said, "The Widget tells me you want to ride round the world on your motorbike."

"That's right."

"Funny, that. Now, I *do* go round the world and all I want to do is to stay put right here."

And that's when the red deer sprang in front of us and Russet chased it.

"We can get down to the river from here," Fred said, leading the way as we clambered and slid down a rock fall. It was rough and stony. Russet was very excited and kept running backwards and forwards to hurry Dizzy Frizzy who was walking as if the stones were hot bricks. Tim and I just sat and slid.

"I'll give you a hand," Fred said to Dinah.

"No, I can manage," she snapped.

The river was full of boulders and the water flowed fast and furious and frightening – to me, anyway. It was deep as there'd been a lot of rain. Fred leapt across and Dad followed but Mum sat down, took out her sketchpad and started to draw as she always does.

"Come on," shouted Dad.

Dizzy Frizzy jumped on to a rock; Russet ran to join her, bark, bark. And in fell Dizzy Frizzy. Suddenly her nose appeared above the water and she dog-paddled really strongly over to Dad and Fred and then back to us.

"She's good," I yelled.

"Poodles are water-dogs," Mum told me. "They swim well."

"Come on," said Fred to Dinah. "I'll look after you."

"Oh, no, you won't," Dinah shouted. "I

can perfectly well look after myself."

Dizzy Frizzy was still swimming in the water and Dinah pushed in Russet to join her.

And it was then we realized what we'd never known before. Russet couldn't swim. She could do everything better than Dizzy Frizzy but she couldn't swim.

"Get her out," Mum yelled, for Dad and Fred were laughing. "She's scared. Get her out!"

Still laughing they pulled her out and Frizzy followed, river water everywhere. Frizzy's white frizzly fur was dripping wet and clung round her funny fat shape.

Russet nipped Frizzy hard to remind her that she was Top Dog even if she couldn't swim and we turned for home as we were starving hungry.

That was our first walk. There were lots more. And all the time we were making discoveries. For the summer we went to live at Goosey was magic – the sun seemed to shine all day long.

Chapter Two

RUSSET IN THE HENHOUSE

Most of the time Russet was a good dog but sometimes she'd get a wicked look in her eyes and then... Look out!

Russet liked to chase hens. When we first came to Goosey Farm we found a chicken hut in the orchard with a low fence surrounding a few hens. Russet just leapt the fence and though we got her out in time we knew then that we'd have to watch her. A new high fence was put up but Mum told us to keep a look-out on our walks, for if she ever came home with a hen clamped between her jaws then we'd all be in trouble.

We'd bought her at a Saturday market where they had a pet stall with mice and rabbits, kittens, hamsters, fish and birds. I wanted her the minute I saw her, sitting on her own, shivering a bit in her smooth chestnut-red coat. She had a wrinkled forehead and gentle eyes. I was with my dad and he bought her and I carried her back home so full of happiness I thought I'd burst.

After Dad went back to sea we moved to Goosey Farm and Aunt Dinah came to live with us. She brought her puppy Dizzy Frizzy, a white miniature poodle, bouncy and squeaky but timid, not like Russet, brave as a lion. Her real name was long and grand, for Dizzy Frizzy was a champion pedigree dog (though she didn't seem much like it).

Russet was a mongrel, but there was a lot of whippet in her, Mum said, which was why she had a streamlined shape and could run like the wind, so Frizzy could never catch her. She kept her red colour as she grew tall and slim.

In the kitchen at Goosey Farm lived Sam Cat's mother. She didn't have a name. We kept giving her one, but we always ended up calling her Sam Cat's Mum. He always tried to gulp down her food as well as his own and gave her a biff every now and then.

"What a dreadful animal that cat is," said Mum, but Dad said Sam was great. Sam Cat's mum had three little kittens, one ginger, one tabby and one black, all in a basket on the stone-flagged floor.

Another member of our family was Charlie the tortoise. He had his name and address written on his shell in Dinah's red nail polish, but the address was where we used to live so it wasn't much use at Goosey.

And we had two grass snakes and some white mice.

Dad hated white mice. He wasn't mad about grass snakes either, one of which had turned up in the bath and grinned at him, he said.

One night Dad came home unexpectedly and as I lay reading on my bed he looked into my room. Suddenly...

"I thought I said you weren't to have any white mice."

"Yes, Dad. You did."

I went on reading, as I'd reached a good bit.

"Well, what's that thing looking at me from the top of your cupboard, then?" he asked, voice very soft and gentle which meant trouble.

A pink nose, ears and whiskers, and bright little eyes were peering and twitching over the end of the wardrobe. Pibbles, as I'd called him, was thinking about jumping down.

"Please can I keep him?" I wailed. "Fred gave him to me. Honest!"

"I'll see. But get him back in that cage. Now!"

I put Pibbles back in the cage with Daisy, the other mouse, and lay thinking about mice hiding places for the next day.

But in the morning Russet wandered into the kitchen, with fat cheeks, and a long pink tail hanging from her mouth.

"She's got Pibbles!" I shouted.

Quick as a flash, Dad seized Russet's nose with one hand and as she opened her jaws he grabbed Pibbles's tail and pulled him out, unharmed and frisky as ever.

I didn't even dare say, "Thank you, Dad."

But he grinned at me and said, "That little feller needs a safer cage. I'll take a look at it for you."

Of course, we ended up with about fifty white mice and finally sold them to a pet shop for money to buy Christmas presents. But that's another story.

*

Fred took us to another part of the river, higher up the valley. He called it the Wallabrook and it was soon our favourite place of all. The Wallabrook starts off as a tiny spring bubbling out of the ground on the High Moor, then flows gurgling, chattering and surging through moorland and rocks to join the river Teign, then tumbles, rushing and growling down, down, down off the moor to meet the sea. Tiny trees grow on the steep banks where daffodils bloom in the spring. We ate our picnic sitting beside and on the clapper bridge, a huge stone boulder thrown across the water, then we played jumping the rocks and the flying water made sparkling rainbows all round us and we got soaked as the dogs splashed us and we fell in from time to time.

Mum sat and drew and Fred talked to Dinah, who mostly just stuck her nose in the air. We all climbed through a huge hole in a stone at the river's edge and then we visited the stone circle nearby. I counted twenty-four standing stones and eight lying down.

"You should come on Midsummer Eve at midnight and run widdershins round the circle and wish," Fred told us.

"That's all rubbish," sniffed Dinah. "You surely don't believe all that."

"What's widdershins?" I asked.

"Opposite way to clockwise. The way witches go."

"Huh," Dinah said.

Russet ran to the middle of the circle, lifted her nose and howled three times. We looked at each other.

"I'm off, back to the bridge," Tim said quickly, "to see if there's any grub left."

But the sausages, crisps, egg

sandwiches, fruit and cake were finished.

Dad wrote a message, put it in a wine bottle and sent it downstream between the rocks and we guessed where it would end up – Antarctica, America, Sahara, China, Africa? He wouldn't tell us what the message was.

At last it was time to go. Tim rode on Dad's shoulders, but I had to walk as we came over the cattle grid, off the moor and on to the path through the fields.

It was hot and I felt tired. It had been a wonderful day but I wanted to be back home.

"It's a long way," I grizzled, dragging behind everyone else with Dizzy Frizzy. Russet was racing ahead as if she could run for ever and ever.

As we went along we saw that a gate into another field stood open. Russet ran towards it.

"Oh, no, come back!" yelled Mum.

"Russet," shouted everyone. "Russet!"

Too late. Russet turned round and looked at us – it was her very wicked look, for in that field there stood a hen hut.

Russet shot into that hut and out of the door jumped one hen, then another hen, then another, four, five, six – all plopped out one by one till at last hen number seven appeared with Russet's jaws in its tail feathers.

Everybody ran to get her, Tim bouncing on Dad's shoulders. But it was Mum who managed to seize Russet's tail.

Dogs absolutely hate, hate, hate having their tails pulled. She swung round to bite Mum and dropped the hen who ran off squawking, quite OK except for a few missing feathers now sticking out of Russet's mouth.

Mum snapped on her lead and we helter-skeltered down the path all the way to Goosey. We were terrified. But no one followed us.

"Bad dog," Dad grumbled when we

were safe home.

"Bad dog," we all told her.

Tail down, ears drooping, sorrow written all over her, Russet got in her box and turned to face the wall. She wouldn't look at us. Every now and then she sighed deeply.

"She's sorry," I said. "Look at her."

"Hm," said Mum. "She is, right now. But she'll do it again if she gets the chance! Bad dog!"

Chapter Three

SKELLYTONS, SPOOKS AND SHEEP

Two brothers, Peter and Christopher, lived at the nearest farm to ours, and we sometimes played with them. But they had been at Stoney Farm all their lives and they frightened us a bit because they knew such a lot and weren't scared of anything. Sometimes they laughed at us, calling us "City Cissies" and "Grockles".

One day Russet disappeared. She was always a busy dog, poking her nose into everything. And she had moods when she didn't want Dizzy Frizzy and would push her away and run off too fast for her to catch up. Frizzy would come back to us, fed up.

When Russet disappeared just before teatime, Frizzy began running round and round, jumping up and whining. She made little rushes at us to get us to go with her. Mum had phoned round but no one had seen Russet. So Tim and I set off at last with Frizzy, who led us to Stoney Farm. Peter and Chris came out and when we told them Russet was missing they said they'd come with us.

"I just hope she hasn't been after hens," Tim whispered to me. "Or she'll be for it."

"Shut up," I whispered. "Don't tell them. She'll be OK. I hope."

Dizzy Frizzy was always a silly sort of dog and now she seemed to be leading us round in circles, but at last she headed off along a wall. And there was a sheep. All on its own. Frizzy froze. She sniffed the air.

"What is this strange creature?" she

seemed to be saying. And then she howled.
I'd never heard Frizzy howl before.

The strange creature went "Baa-aa-aa"
and Frizzy put her little stumpy tail between
her legs and rushed behind me in terror.
The sheep turned round and pushed its way
through a gap in the wall. Dizzy Frizzy put
her nose into my hand. She was trembling.

Peter and Christopher fell about
laughing.

"Scared of a sheep, ha ha. Scared of a sheep, ho ho."

"Shut up," Tim shouted. "*You'd* be scared in a city. There are burglars and things."

"You can be scared of burglars. But a sheep. A sheep. Not much of a dog, is it?"

I took no notice and soon Frizzy rushed ahead as if she knew exactly where she was going.

"Anyway there's worse on the moor than burglars," Peter went on.

"What?" I snapped.

"Ghosts and monsters and the Whish hounds and devils and giants."

"Oh, them. They're just *legends*."

"No, they're not, Widget. There's a really haunted place just near here and I bet the evil spirit that lives there has *got* Russet, 'cos that's where Frizzy's taking us, you'll see."

"You mean...?"

"Yes, that one that looks like a

mushroom!"

"Yes, you can just *see* it's haunted. I bet Russet went there 'cos she's nosy and its secret power pulled her into its centre and sacrificed her!"

"Sacrificed her?"

"Yeah, they used to have sacrifices there. Human and animal! Blood on the stones! That's what we'll find," said Christopher.

"It's an Ancient Burial Chamber, you see," said Peter.

"I know. Mum told me. We went to look at it."

Three granite slabs stood in a field with one plonked on top built long, long ago in the Neolithic stone age, she said, by our ancestors. A metal notice read,

ANCIENT MONUMENT
BURIAL CHAMBER
3000 YEARS OLD

I didn't think it was spooky. Then. Now the shadows were growing longer. And I was afraid. I was afraid for Russet and I was afraid for us. I didn't want us all to be sacrifices.

"Let's go back," Tim said.

"No, come on. We've got to find her. Russet, Russet!" I shouted.

We all ran, Dizzy Frizzy going really fast, looking over her shoulder at us and yapping her squeaky bark.

We reached the field with the Ancient Monument, woods looming all round the edges. Through the gate we hurtled, Peter turning round to close it.

"Russet! Russet!" we called as we headed for the monument.

"Look! There's something in those bushes over there," cried Tim.

He pointed. There was something – red lights flashed and a...

Tim grabbed my hand and screamed, "It's a skellyton. And it's coming for us."

It was. Red eyes in a horrible white face came out from the bushes, pale and glowing because it was now dark.

"Run! Run!" I shouted.

"Help!" shouted Peter.

"Run for it," yelled Christopher.

Back to the gate we headed as fast as we could go. But the skeleton head followed us.

"It's a death's-head!" yelled Tim.

Panting, near tears, we ran and ran. But the death's-head floated along even faster, silently, terrifyingly. No body. Just a head.

Suddenly there was just one stone too many. Tim fell over. I crouched over him, arms outstretched, terrified, ready to fight the monster now on top of us.

And at that moment Russet leapt on me,

licking me furiously.

"It's Russet!"

Both dogs were barking excitedly. But there was another with them, wagging its tail.

Tim stood up.

"The monster's only a dog!"

"He won't hurt us. Look, he's a friendly dog!" cried Peter.

"What, with a head like that?" Tim gasped.

He was a big dog with a thick black furry coat, a completely smooth white head and red eyes. In the dark all we'd seen were the shining head and glowing eyes.

"It must be dangerous," Tim said. "It looks like a ghost dog."

"Russet likes him so he can't be a ghost dog, can he?"

I didn't care. I was too busy hugging my friend, my very best friend, Russet. She was safe.

"But you're a naughty dog," I whispered in her springy ears.

The naughty dog gave a huge deep sigh and wagged her tail as we hurried home.

The monster came all the way back to the farm with us and we gave him a bone which he chewed just inside the kitchen door. After a while he stood up and whined. He wanted to go home. We opened the door and he trotted away.

He came back the next day and every next day – usually at different times. Peter and Chris told us he lived on Mr Mudge's farm about five miles away and his real name was Spot.

"He doesn't look like a Spot," Tim said. "I'm going to call him Death's-head."

So we did.

Death's-head was our friend now. He liked you to throw sticks or a ball for him and he'd bring them back, wagging and waggling wildly. Russet obviously thought he was crazy. If you threw her anything she just went off with it.

Death's-head loved all of us but especially Russet. If she growled or snapped at him he would tremble, sink down to the ground, drop his tail and put his paws over his red eyes that looked so wicked and were really so gentle, for he was a soppy dog.

He had one enemy. Sam Cat hated him. He could put up with Russet and Frizzy because they were ours and belonged with us. But Death's-head didn't. Sam Cat certainly didn't want this great big ugly dog about the farm. He used to lurk high up on branches and roofs, then drop down on Death's-head with all claws out and Death's-head would yowl and rush round crazily with Sam on his back.

Chapter Four

GROCKLES AT GOOSEY

The school we went to only had thirty-five children. Our old school had had five hundred. I was in the Junior class taught by the Head Teacher, Mrs Cotter, and Tim was in the Infants with Miss Partridge. Lots of people came in to help and we had a school orchestra and a choir and we were going to do a play about David and Goliath for Open Day. Mrs Cotter picked me for David. First of all I was pleased and then I wasn't, because a girl called Caroline was mad about it.

"Why pick her?" she asked. "She's only

just come. She's a Grockle from the city. Not fair. And David ought to be a boy."

"She's little and she's got a big voice," Mrs Cotter said firmly. "She'll do very nicely for David. We don't have to have a boy for the part. John Ellis, you can be Goliath."

John Ellis was the tallest, biggest boy in the school, bigger than Mrs Cotter even. He lived on a farm on the High Moor and brought in wonderful flowers and strange things for the Nature table. He was supposed to have a tame hawk at home and he could ride any horse or pony no matter how wild. Mrs Cotter said he knew more about the countryside than she did. He didn't talk much and he hadn't spoken to me at all.

Chris and Peter Stone were friendly when we were at home with the animals but at school they took no notice of us and I felt lonely, especially with Tim in the other classroom. Caroline whispered something to Chris.

"They're not real farmers," Chris said out loud so that everyone could hear, "even if they do live at Goosey. Their dad's a sailor and their mum draws pictures for books. You see. They're not *real* people. They're just Grockles."

Caroline said to me, "Bet you won't stay here long."

"Why not?" I asked.

"You won't be able to stand the winters. I hope you go soon."

"Why? What have we done to you?"

"Your Aunt Dinah's pinched my sister's boyfriend."

"What? Fred? She doesn't even like him. She didn't pinch him. She doesn't want him."

"We don't want you either," she hissed at me. "Coming here and sneaking the best part in the play."

Chris was grinning and I felt so hurt I wanted to cry but I wasn't going to. Then from behind me a voice said,

"Leave 'er be, Caroline Bovey, and shut up. She didn't ask for the part and people 'as a right to be different. Look 'ow animals and birds is different. So can people be. Just leave 'er be or you'll 'ave me to settle with. So shut up." It was John Ellis.

Caroline shut up.

At the end of the afternoon – it was a Friday – Mrs Cotter read us a story about how important it was to be friends and we were all quiet as we went out of school. But as I came out of the cloakroom I heard Caroline say to the girls, "You'll have to leave *her* alone. She's teacher's pet and John Ellis's girlfriend."

I was glad it was Saturday next day and Dad was coming home for the weekend. I hadn't known we were so different. I didn't even want to be in the play. John Ellis scared me and besides I didn't want to be anyone's girlfriend. It was Russet I loved best, and I told her all about it in bed that night.

Then the news at breakfast on Saturday morning made me forget all about school, plays and everything.

"Russet's going to have puppies," Mum said. We went crazy, jumping and leaping about. Puppies! Puppies! I was over the moon.

"When? When? Can we keep them? I'll have to think up names for them. Oh Russet! Russet! She'll be fat. How fat will she be? How many will there be?"

Mum was laughing.

"You'll have to wait and see."

And she wouldn't say any more than that.

Something else happened that weekend. Something to do with Sam Cat and the Goosey Farm mice.

Sam Cat was very busy these days. We didn't see much of him except when he came on walks with us. When we first came to Goosey with its old rooms we saw and heard lots of mice and ... bigger creatures. At night you could hear little feet running behind the Elizabethan panelling. So Sam Cat knew his time had come. Here was his kingdom!

The larder was dark and old and it soon became clear that the mice were having midnight feasts. Mum was disgusted and scrubbed out everything, but they came back so she put down mousetraps. Tim cried but she was firm.

"I hate mousetraps too but it's them or us!" Mum said.

Next morning I crept in, fearing to see little dead bodies but the mousetraps had gone. Whatever had visited the larder was big enough to take the traps away with it! That night I heard little feet running behind the panelling and a dragging noise like a sledge.

"They're monster rats!" cried Tim.

"Get Sam Cat," Mum said.

Sam Cat got going and soon no more running feet were heard at night. For Sam

Cat ruled OK. He sorted out Goosey Farm. He grew very big and walked round as if he owned the place. He purred loudly when you stroked him.

"You can count on me. I shall look after you," he seemed to be saying. (Well, except for Death's-head.)

Chapter Five

PICNIC TIME

"Summertime, and the livin' is easy," warbled Mum. She was right. It was the half-term holiday. Dad had a week's leave, Granny and Grandad had come to stay, Dinah's old boyfriend, Andy, had turned up, the farm was full and we were going on a picnic that afternoon, for it was going to be a beautiful day.

Mum and I had crept out early that morning because she wanted to get her drawings done before she had to look after everybody. She was illustrating a book on water animals and plants so we were down

by the river. Russet and Dizzy
Frizzy had come too. You couldn't
slip out of the house without them knowing.
I liked it when I was with Mum on her own.

"You could put Frizzy in that book.
She's a water creature," I said as she jumped,
plop, into the river. Russet stood on the
bank watching her, looking angry.

"She's funny-tempered these days."

"It's the puppies," Mum replied. "Besides, she's always jealous when Frizzy swims, because she can't."

But just then Death's-head arrived and he and Russet chased each other up and down the river bank.

★

Granny and Grandad had news of all our old friends. It sounded strange hearing about what they were doing.

"Don't you miss it all?" Granny asked Mum.

"Only sometimes when it rains all day or the mist comes down over the moor."

"I love it then. It's all mysterious like in an adventure," I said.

"So you really like it here?" Granny went on. "Honestly?"

"Honestly, yes. But I don't seem to have many friends ..."

"It's early days," put in Mum.

"... because I haven't made many friends at school yet."

"I have," said Tim, joining in. "Lots."

"Oh, you ..."

We took Granny and Grandad to all our favourite places and we had a smashing picnic. Peter and Chris came too because they were friendly when we weren't at school. We explored the moor around the Wallabrook and then we went to Kes Tor and gazed at the moor stretching for miles and miles and miles. Dad showed us the prehistoric remains where people had lived hundred of years ago.

"Here's one of the prehistoric men," giggled Chris as Fred suddenly appeared from behind a huge granite rock and headed straight for Dinah, who was just finishing off a bottle of wine that Andy had brought for her, along with flowers and chocolates and perfume, for Dinah always gets lots of presents. I crept nearer to listen, taking no notice of Mum who shook her head at me.

Dinah was all pink and giggly (from the wind and the wine, I heard Dad say).

"Won't you introduce me?" asked Andy, who sounded rather posh.

"Whom you got 'ere with 'ee, then?" asked Fred in his best dialect.

He looked as if he'd been muck-

spreading in his old cords.

"Perhaps they'll have a scrap," Tim whispered.

"I'll put my money on Fred," Dad whispered back.

"Andy, meet Fred. Fred, this is Andy."

They glared at each other, both red in the face.

"Come on," Dad shouted. "I think it's time we were getting back home."

We ran down the hill to where the cars were parked. Fred and Andy shot ahead of the rest of us, racing one another. I didn't see what happened but suddenly Andy was sprawling in a mud patch, his designer jeans filthy.

"Oh, dear," Fred grinned. "I'll help you. It can be dangerous round here."

But Dinah coming up behind gave him a push and he joined Andy in a heap. I left them to it and ran on with Russet and Frizzy. So did Dinah.

*

Later we all tucked into an enormous spread in the kitchen. Peter and Chris stayed too.

"Your mum's a good cook," said Peter, spluttering puff-pastry bits everywhere.

"My dad did most of it," I spluttered back. "He likes cooking. So there."

Later Chris looked at the animal pictures on the walls.

"Hey, they're triffic."

"My mum did them."

"She's good."

"Even if she's only a Grockle?" I asked.

It was a wonderful holiday. Every day we went somewhere new and at night we settled into the old farm which wrapped itself around us like a blanket. I was trying to draw like Mum, though I wasn't nearly as good as she was, and Tim was learning to play with the computer Dad had brought home with him. He'd got some ideas running round in his head, he said. I imagined them like the mice behind our panelling.

Dinah went on teasing Andy. Fred kept turning up and she'd sit on the wooden settle with the two of them glaring at each other from either side.

"You'll have to choose between them," Dad told her later.

"No, I won't. I shall do as I please. I *like* the new job I've got here and I don't want to *choose* anyone. So there."

"I'd choose Fred any day," I told Russet and Frizzy in bed. "He's miles better than that wimpy Andy."

Grandad gave me and Tim a nice lot of money when they left.

"I'm glad you're happy, my dear, and doing your painting," he said to Mum.

"It's lovely here," Granny told us. "But— but I wonder what it's like in winter? And when Joe's at sea for a long time?"

"We'll just have to wait and see!" Mum laughed.

Chapter Six

FRIZZY IN DANGER

Slowly – too slowly it seemed to us – Russet grew fat, but only in her tum. She was as thin as a pin otherwise so she did look a bit funny.

"Like a dog spider," Tim said.

Russet didn't like her new shape much. Her head now looked tiny compared with her fat tum and she'd turn it from side to side, trying to find out what had happened to her, and she'd lick bits she could reach to see if she could get it all the right shape again. Worst of all, Frizzy could now run faster than Russet could and when we went

on walks she'd go ahead. If this happened too often Russet would nip the back of her legs.

But it was a happy time, for we wanted the puppies more than anything.

"We'll have to watch out for Sam Cat," Mum said a few weeks later. "I hope he likes them."

It was already clear that Sam Cat *didn't* like Death's-head, who turned up at Goosey Farm nearly every day now.

"Keeping an eye on his puppies-to-be," Mum said.

"No! He can't be the father," I cried.

"Why not?"

"All the puppies will be *hideous*! He's so ugly."

"Not necessarily. They'll probably look like Russet."

"Oh, I hope so. Fancy, Death's-head puppies!"

Death's-head then decided to sniff Sam Cat's bottom as dogs do. Sam Cat was furious. He jumped round like a boxer and delivered a quick one-two, all claws out sharp to Death's-head's big nose.

Death's-head ran yelping down the path. We didn't see him for the rest of the day or the next one.

But on Saturday he came trotting back, sure of his welcome. Russet was curled up in the porch with Frizzy. No one spotted Sam Cat on the porch roof. Just as Death's-head was almost grinning at the sight of Russet, Sam Cat leapt off the porch directly on to Death's-head's white bony head and stuck in his wicked sharp claws as hard as he could.

Death's-head's howl was terrible. Mum came belting up the garden to see what catastrophe had befallen Goosey, only to find Death's-head galloping round and round like a mad horse with a demon rider on its back. The last we saw was the pair of them careering down the lane at top speed, both howling and screaming.

"They'll be all right," Mum told Tim. "Don't worry, they'll sort it out in their own way."

Sam Cat returned but Death's-head didn't come back for a week while Sam Cat wandered round with a smirk on his face.

"After all, I *am* the Boss Cat," he seemed to be saying.

At school we were practising for Open Day all the time now. The orchestra played, the choir sang and we rehearsed *David and Goliath*. And I was nervous. Caroline played the part of a Jewish maiden and she watched me out of slitty eyes. But nothing was said. For though John Ellis didn't speak to me any more than he ever had, he always seemed to be around and now I was never teased.

Mrs Cotter read us a poem about a cat at the end of the afternoon. It was a super poem and suddenly, before I had time to think, I said,

"It would be great if someone read it

on Open Day."

"Yes," said Mrs Cotter. "It would. Who could read it then?"

"Caroline," I said as fast as anything. "She'd be perfect."

"Good idea. You try it, Caroline."

She read it perfectly.

"She's just like a cat," said her friend, Celia. "It suits her."

"Yes, I'll put that in the programme," Mrs Cotter said. "You can dress up in a cat outfit, Caroline. Would you like that?"

I crossed my fingers.

"Yes," she purred. Well, it sounded like purring. I uncrossed my fingers. After school she came up to me.

"I've got some mints. D'you want one?" And she smiled.

"Yes, please." And I smiled back.

And then, I saw Mum with Russet and Frizzy come to meet us out of school. But Frizzy, Dizzy Frizzy, mad Frizzy, crazy

Frizzy, Frizzy who never had any sense to
her, suddenly slipped her lead and ran
straight to us just as the school bus was

rolling into position to pick up the children who lived far away.

I screamed, "Frizzy, Frizzy. Don't!"

But too late. She was right under the wheels and Tim, yelling, jumped under the bus to save her. It all happened so quickly. I stood shell-shocked, screaming. But Chris Stone, my friend/enemy, dived like a swimmer under the bus, rolled over and pulled Tim to safety while Frizzy ran out unhurt.

Everyone cheered. But Chris didn't wait to hear. Beetroot red, he turned and ran for home as fast as he could.

Chapter Seven
PUPPY SPECIAL

One morning we were walking to school, which meant going through the garden and the orchard, over the stile and along a footpath leading to the lane. It was a short-cut and Mum often walked the dogs along with us. That morning Russet seemed restless, and kept stopping to lick herself.

"She won't be long now," Mum told us. "She went all round the house last night looking for a place to have them."

"I hope she picks my bed," Tim said.

"Not likely. She'll have them in her box. I've put an old holey blanket in there."

It was hard for Russet to get through the stile and soon she stood still in the field and wouldn't go any further. Tim and Frizzy were running ahead but I stopped with Mum and Russet. She was panting and pushing and suddenly out popped a soft transparent little sack just like a polythene bag and inside there was a shape ...

Russet started licking it.

"She's having her babies here in the field," cried Mum. "Come on."

"What can we do? She can't have them here!"

"She can. She is."

Tim ran back. Frizzy bounced up and down like a yo-yo.

Mum seized the little thing still half in its sack and I caught a glimpse of the new puppy.

"She's the same colour as Russet!"

Mum pulled off her cardigan.

"Carry it. Carefully now."

She wrapped up the puppy and I hurried as fast as I could keeping everything steady, Tim carrying all the school things and talking his head off, Frizzy running round our legs as excited as we were. Mum picked up Russet, we headed for the house, up the field, over the stile, through the garden. I thought we'd never get to the kitchen but when we did Russet got into her box and I carefully put the puppy beside her. She started to wash it as it struggled out of its little sack and began to feed. The other puppies popped out one after another and Russet cleaned them up and sorted them out. Mum gave her a drink on a saucer and soon they were all feeding happily, with all of us crouched around. Frizzy tried to lick one of the puppies but Russet growled angrily and she sat quietly, subdued at last.

"Don't be jealous, Frizzy," I said, patting her.

The first puppy was the only one that looked like Russet. She was already beautiful. The others were super – there were six altogether – but very funny.

"They look like baby hippos," Tim said.

And they did. We couldn't stop watching them so, of course, we didn't want to go to school that day.

But we had to. And we were late. The teachers gathered all the children round us and we told them about the puppies.

"We've had lots of puppies at *our* farm," said Chris but he grinned at me.

John Ellis spoke.

"I'd like to come and see them," was what he said.

"Oh, yes," I agreed.

Russet always growled if Frizzy came too near her puppies and this made Frizzy sad.

"Never mind," Mum said. "You shall

have some of your own one day when you're a big dog. But yours will be pedigree puppies. Not like Russet's."

"They're beautiful," I protested.

And they were. Even if five of them did look like baby hippos.

Chapter Eight

SAM CAT THE PROTECTOR

Open Day arrived. Dad couldn't be there but Mum and Dinah came wearing dresses for once and looking beautiful, so I felt very proud. Russet and Frizzy had been left at home.

The parents looked at our work, tried out our cooking and watched the P.E. display. The History project table was very good but the Nature table was out of this world.

Then the orchestra tuned up. I played the recorder and Tim the triangle. We sang our songs and the poems came next.

Caroline did hers wonderfully. She had a velvety suit with ears, whiskers and tail.

Next on the programme was the play *David and Goliath*. As David, I wore a bit of sacking and carried a catapult. I didn't feel sure of myself at all. I thought I looked silly and I still wished they'd chosen someone else. But John Ellis stood giant high in the armour he'd made in Art and Technology.

I was very nervous. But when I came on and said I'd challenge Goliath to do battle I

wasn't nervous any more and felt I could do *anything*. You could almost feel the silence as I fitted my sling and took aim.

John Ellis fell down flat, all his armour clanging and banging. He lay as still as if he really was dead.

Everyone clapped for ages. I could see Mum beaming and Dinah as well. After we'd done our bows lots of people came up to me and said kind things.

"Lovely curls you have," said one lady.

"Just my idea of David."

"I never wanted curls," I muttered. "Don't like them much."

"Your boy was good," said another mum to mine.

"Can I come see your puppies soon?" John Ellis whispered to me, "to make up for you killing me!"

"Yeh," I answered. I didn't dare say no. He was twice my size.

"What a wonderful day!" said my mum as we made our way home. "You both did very well."

Soon afterwards we broke up for the summer holidays. Summer holidays at Goosey, oh, wow!

The puppies grew bigger, fatter and more wriggly and playful. Frizzy was allowed to puppy-sit now as Russet sometimes got fed up with them and wanted to be on her own. I cleaned up puddles and stopped them getting stuck in places, for their fat tums were wider than their little legs. They liked to have their tums rubbed and they smelled of biscuits and licked everything, especially faces. They all had names – Porker, Baggins, Agatha, Fred, Lulu and Hanna, the first puppy, Red Hanna, the one I loved best. She was like Russet, but gentler somehow. My Hanna.

In the long summer
evenings we'd line them up
and they'd run races, and we laughed
because they rolled over and turned round
and forgot what they were doing. Relatives
and friends came to stay with us; we had lots
of picnics and outings with Russet and
Frizzy and Death's-head (and Sam Cat
following behind). Dinah kept changing
boyfriends so there was often someone new.
But Fred was always around. Dad came
home every weekend.

We ate wild strawberries and fruit and
vegetables from the garden. Chris and Peter
were our real friends now.

Walking along barefoot one day with the
dogs we saw a posh car driving slowly past.
A head stuck out of the window.

"Goodness, they must be natives, poor
things."

So we jumped up and down yelling like
Tarzan and pretending to be monkeys.

"We're not Grockles any more," I told

Tim. "We're natives. We live here."

Summer changed slowly to autumn. Mornings were misty and evenings came early. The leaves were turning and soon we'd be going back to school. Midges covered me with bites. Tim was stung by a wasp. Sam Cat's mum's kittens had long gone to good homes and Mum said she'd fix up the puppies with homes when they were old enough, quite soon now.

"John Ellis hasn't been to see them yet," I cried.

"Well, they're not going yet, but you must ring him to come and see them."

I sat in the barn and thought about this.

"What are you crying for?" Tim asked.

"I don't want them to go. I don't want things to change. Not ever. And I'm not crying. I don't cry."

I couldn't be brave enough to ring John Ellis and he didn't come.

We had the biggest draining board in the world at Goosey, a huge wooden one made for giants.

One morning Sam Cat sat on it, very still, head down. His front paw was torn and bleeding, the worst wound we'd ever seen on Sam. The vet came and shook his head.

"He's had a terrible fight with some creature," he said. The paw was bathed and Sam injected with penicillin. He lay motionless in his box, Russet and Frizzy

keeping guard. We fussed over him – Sam
Cat, who hated fuss – but he was too ill to
notice.

Tim and I went searching. We searched
in the bedrooms, in the downstairs rooms, in
the strange wild garden, in the outhouses
and the barns. We didn't know what we
were looking for but we knew it when we
found it. For in one of the barns lay the torn

and mangled body of a weasel, a fierce wild animal with sharp teeth. It was covered with scratches and bites and quite dead. Sam Cat had kept his promise to look after us. Sam had fought for us and nearly died.

Sam Cat lived, though only just. It took him a long time to get better and when he did he'd changed. Sam Cat the Hunter was no more. He turned into a quiet and gentle cat who slept his time away, purring gently when stroked. Sometimes I wondered what he dreamt of as he dozed in the sun or in the warmth of the fire. Did he remember his great days when he was Boss Cat of Goosey Farm?

Chapter Nine

NOW THE SUMMER ENDS

"Come on," cried Mum. "You're back at school tomorrow. It's a beautiful morning. Let's make the most of it!"

So off we scrambled down to the river early that September morning.

"Look!" shouted Tim, after a while. "Look, Russet's swimming. She can swim!"

She was too. Lifting her nose high out of the water, she dog-paddled along, in a slow, stately manner, looking comical but we didn't laugh, oh, no. She clambered up the bank at last, shaking spots of water madly

and waggling at Frizzy dancing round her, both of them pleased as Punch.

"We'll go home the long way. I've a call to make," said Mum.

Off we trotted. All was very still, very quiet. At last we turned off the path and into the lane, nearly home.

"We ought to put them on their leads," I said.

"It's early. There's no one about," Mum said, looking down the lane. "They'll be all right. Russet's so pleased with herself."

And round the bend came a car, not even going fast. But the bumper caught Russet on the head and she lay in the dust, not marked at all, her beautiful coat shining red-gold. I held her and held her till someone came and took her away. I could not believe that Russet could be dead. Not Russet. Russet couldn't ever be dead.

Chapter Ten
SAYING GOODBYE

I didn't know grown-ups cried so much. I
thought my mother would never stop. Tim
comforted her and Dinah comforted her but
it was no good. She wouldn't stop crying
But I couldn't talk to her. There was a wall
between us. She'd never been any good at
putting on leads and because of this Russet,
my best friend, lay buried on the moor and I
should never again see her running like the
wind, her red coat shining. So I didn't want
to talk to my mother.

   I sat in a barn with the puppies. Frizzy
was curled in a sad little heap as they played.

A shadow darkened the doorway. It was too big for Tim, it must be Fred. I looked up. It was John Ellis. He sat on the barn floor and the puppies ran all over him, licking and wriggling. He didn't say anything but then he hardly ever did. We just sat there in the barn. Death's-head came in and licked him. Then Death's-head licked one of the puppies, lifted up his head and howled three times just as Russet had in the stone circle, long ago. It was a dreadful sound. And I began to cry at last.

John Ellis picked up little red Hanna and put her on my lap.

"She'll be your Russet," he said. "Don't cry."

Then he pointed to the fattest and ugliest puppy, Baggins.

"When you're ready, I'll have this one," he said. "Bye, Widget. See you around."

He and Death's-head left together.

At last Dad came.

"No need to cry," he said. "Russet's chasing hens in paradise."

"Not much of a paradise for the hens," Mum choked, but she'd looked up and was listening.

"Well, you see, they've been very wicked hens so they've got to be chased by Russet until they've improved enough to go to a hen paradise."

She started to smile – not much of one – but a smile. At last she spoke.

"I know," she said. "I'll paint a picture of her running on the moor."

But it was Frizzy who fretted most for Russet. Her ears dropped, her tail drooped, she wouldn't eat. She didn't jump or squeak. She grew thin and lay all day curled up in her basket watching the door in case Russet came. At last Mum and Dinah decided that the only thing to save her would be puppies of her own.

"I know someone who breeds poodles

but she lives on the other side of the moor," said Dinah.

I saw them look at one another and when we came home from school the next day Frizzy had gone.

Aunt Dinah had arranged for Frizzy to go there. The woman said she'd keep Frizzy for a bit and see how she got on, at least till spring, and if she seemed happier there would let her stay. Mum's face pleaded with me. She couldn't let Frizzy go on pining at home. Maybe her memories of Russet were *too* painful.

Tim ran at Dinah and hit her but then they both cried.

"I'm going too," Dinah sobbed. "I've quarrelled with Fred... Really quarrelled, I mean. And I've packed in my job. I was rude to a customer who made passes at me!"

"You'll get another boyfriend. And another job."

"I don't *want* another boyfriend. And they've written and offered me my old job back – so I'm going home tomorrow!"

Next day Dinah left.

Summer had gone for good. Gales roared across the moor, bringing rain and hail. Mr Stone, Peter's and Chris's father, came to fetch the puppies.

"They're going to good homes," Mum said. But I wouldn't speak to her, just picked up Hanna and the one John Ellis wanted and hid them in the furthest barn in case Mum decided to send them away as well. I was still angry with her.

"It's all her fault, even this horrible weather!" I muttered in Hanna's ear. She licked mine in return. "But at least Dad's coming home this weekend."

Dad came and we did lots of jobs on the house, fixing bolts and checking doors and windows. Even then we didn't guess.

But that evening he told us he was leaving at the end of the week. This time he would be away for six months at least.

"I'll see you in the summer!" He tried to comfort us.

"What summer?" I asked.

Down poured the rain, on and on, day after day. The moor was dark and menacing. We splashed to school. Mum drew pictures for a children's book this time. Hanna grew. She did look like Russet but somehow she wasn't funny like Russet and Frizzy had been. Or maybe we weren't funny any more.

Chapter Eleven

MISTLETOE AND MUSIC

It seemed very quiet at Goosey Farm with Frizzy, Dad and Dinah and the puppies gone and Sam Cat grown suddenly old and no Russet, but you can't go on sorrowing forever.

There came a day when the sun shone and we ran over the moor with Hanna, shouting our heads off, bringing home berries for Mum to stand in the big stone vase. Mum's book was lovely, the best she'd ever done, she hoped. Dad sent long letters with funny stories about life at sea. Friends came to see us and Mr Stone and Fred helped Mum a lot. So did Tim and me. We stacked up logs and filled the freezer ready for a Dartmoor winter. We went for lots of walks.

Best of all was school. I couldn't believe that once I'd not had any friends there. Now everyone was my friend, especially Caroline. I was known as John Ellis's girlfriend though he never actually spoke to me in school, but it did mean I never got left out or laughed at. We were invited to birthday parties and everyone came to Tim's in November when we had fireworks, baked potatoes, sausages and roasted chestnuts. Caroline and I were asked to a birthday party at a funny old lady's home, where there was just a blue cake with one candle on it. The old lady played on a twangy old piano and we had to sing with her. She gave us a bunch of dried flowers when we came away.

She liked us very much, she said. But the house and the old lady were very strange and I was glad when my mum and Caroline's turned up to collect us.

John Ellis unpeeled himself off a tree in the garden as we left. Baggins, his puppy, wagged his tail when he saw me. He was getting to be much bigger than Hanna now.

"What were you doing there?" asked Mum.

"Keeping an eye on things, like," he said.

Caroline nudged me with her elbow but I took no notice. "You're being looked after," she said.

We did a Christmas concert at school. I was learning to play the clarinet and Tim the recorder. It was OK.

So Christmas arrived at last. Granny and Grandad came and so did Dinah, on her own. We decorated the tree and hung holly everywhere. There were lots of presents for everyone and a box from Dad, full of strange and crazy things like his always were. Hanna grew very excited and chased round and round. Granny and Grandad were jolly.

"You two are quiet," Grandad said to Mum and Dinah.

"No, we're not."

"Yes, you are. You're missing *your men*."

"No, I'm not," shouted Dinah. And in walked Fred, looking smart in a suit!

"I've brought some mistletoe," he grinned, holding it above her head.

"Don't you dare!" she cried and ran

away upstairs. Soon they were chasing
round and round the two staircases with all
the rest of us joining in, even Grandad...

But in bed that night I told Hanna all
about her mother and I showed her the

photo of Frizzy that had arrived, a fat Frizzy who was going to have puppies. Hanna got hold of it before I could stop her and chewed half of it to pieces.

"Bad dog," I grumbled. "You're a bad dog, just like your mother."

She wagged her tail.

But I couldn't help feeling sad. It had been a nice Christmas but with no Dad, no Russet and no Frizzy it couldn't be perfect.

Hanna pushed her nose into my hand and looked at me.

"I'm here. Won't I do? You've got to forget my mother and think of *me*," she seemed to say.

Two days after Christmas is my birthday and we invited my best friends from school. They all came: Caroline, Celia, Grace and Natasha, Chris and Peter and their cousins who were staying with them, John Ellis with Baggins.

We ate tons of food and played mad games, Twister, Dead Lions, Consequences and Murder. Red Hanna and Baggins dashed everywhere and even Sam Cat woke up a bit.

"You ought to kiss John Ellis under the mistletoe," whispered Caroline to me.

"No way. I'm like Dinah. I don't want boyfriends."

"Well, just you look in the other room."

"Why?"

"Just you look," grinned Caroline.

We peeped in the sitting room. Fred and Dinah were kissing one another like crazy but funnily enough there wasn't a bit of mistletoe in sight.

We stood at the doorway saying goodnight to everybody. The stars sparkled in the sky and it was very cold. An icy wind stirred and blew over us.

"Look out," said Mr Stone to Mum. "It'll be a sharp frost tonight. And snow is forecast."

"We'll be getting on our way tomorrow," Grandad said.

"So will I," Dinah added.

"Aren't you staying then?" asked Fred.

"Certainly not. Whatever for?" answered Dinah.

Chapter Twelve

WHEN THE SNOW CAME

Later the next day, after Granny and Grandad and Dinah had driven away, it grew very cold and the sky hung like a curtain. We took Hanna for a quick walk, then we fastened up Goosey Farm for the night. Mr Stone had warned Mum to have shovels and spades and brooms handy in case of bad weather.

"I hope it snows and snows up to the roof so we don't have to go back to school," said Tim.

We settled in quietly that night and read our Christmas books and played with our

Christmas games. I really hoped it would snow. I'd never seen a deep snow and I wondered what it would be like as I snuggled down with Hanna into my bed.

"It's really, really cold," I whispered to her.

The room looked strange, different when I woke up, filled with a weird light. I ran to the window and looked out but couldn't see anything, for the window was covered with white blobs.

"Mum! Tim! Come on, come on! It's snowing!" Hanna bounced round my feet, catching my excitement.

Mum was already up, cooking breakfast.

"I don't want any."

"Yes, you do. You're going to need your breakfast. We've got paths to clear and work to do."

We gobbled our breakfasts and grabbed clothes and boots. But when we opened the kitchen door the snow was already as high as Tim and it was still falling steadily, white

and cold. We tried to dig it away from the door but the flakes continued to fall from the grey sky, filling any space we managed to clear.

"Mum, it's not like I thought it would be. I don't like it much."

"No, this is serious, not fun. Come on, let's build up a really warm fire and settle in till it stops snowing. You can't go out in this."

Snow fell silently, endlessly all through the day, all through the night. It fell all that day and night, drifting higher and higher around the windows and walls of the old farm. I watched from a window as the flakes whirled and wheeled in every direction out of the heavy snow-laden sky, adding to the white blanket already covering Goosey Farm. Downstairs it was so cold that you had to sit really close to the Aga cooker to keep warm. The three of us, Mum, Tim and I, sat with Hanna and the cats. I felt very strange.

About three o'clock in the afternoon it seemed like the middle of the night.

Shortly afterwards we heard a knocking and a banging. Tim looked scared but it turned out to be Fred who walked in the door with John Ellis.

"We've come while we can to see if you're all right," they said.

We made them sit down and have a warm drink and some food. It was so good to see them and know that we weren't alone in a world turned to snow.

"What can we do?"

"Nothing till it stops. Stay in and keep warm. Have you got some candles and some tins of food?"

"Yes— you mean..."

"The power will go off if the lines come down and you'll have no lights. If it lasts you'll have to put the food from the freezer out in the snow!" Fred said.

"We can manage," Mum said.

"Well, take care of yourself. Specially now," said Fred and gave her a kiss.

John Ellis hadn't said a word but as he left he pushed a bar of chocolate at me.

"Snow rations," he muttered.

"Mum," I asked when they'd gone and Tim and I had eaten the chocolate. "What did Fred mean by 'specially now'?"

"Oh! Nothing," she said. "Come on, let's play one of the new games Grandad gave us."

That winter Dartmoor was shown on all the newsreels, the worst snowfall for years. Power lines were down. There were no phones, no electricity. Helicopters dropped hay for the sheep and ponies, fed and rescued people on isolated farms, flew people who were ill or injured and pregnant women to hospital. Pictures showed mile after mile of drifting white Arctic fields and woods and villages and houses that were cut off. Only those in the middle of it didn't see it, for nothing was working. We were imprisoned indoors with candles and tins of beans and the Aga.

Time and us, we'd split.

Late one afternoon the snow stopped and the wind dropped and the sun shone in a suddenly clear blue sky. The snow froze and, where it had drifted, strange shapes seemed to be carved by an ice sculptor.

Overhead the helicopters roared, searching, searching, endlessly searching.

"There's something at the door," Tim whispered. "It sounds scary."

Mum was resting, she said. She slept a lot these days.

"I'll go," I said. "Wait there."

I opened the heavy front door. The snow had drifted into the porch where Russet and Frizzy used to sit in the sunshine.

Something was there. Something was trying to jump up. It was a funny shape, covered with icicles and it couldn't really jump.

Then this strange apparition squeaked.
And I knew that squeak.

"Frizzy!" I screamed. "Dizzy Frizzy!"

I'd got her in my arms and she was
trying to lick my face with her tiny cold
tongue. She felt frozen so it went right
through my thick sweater.

I carried her in shouting and calling,
"Mum, Tim," and crying my eyes out as I'd

never cried for Russet. "Come on. Come on. It's Frizzy. Oh, come on. She's so cold she'll die. And she's full of babies. Oh, Frizzy, I love you, Frizzy. Come, come. Come and see. Get some warm milk, Tim — just a drop. And a blanket. And a hot-water bottle. We've got to get her warm. Her fur's all frozen. Frozen, frozen Frizzy."

My mother's a wonder for crying. She was down on her knees, hugging Frizzy who was licking her face as if she was trying to empty the ocean my mother was trying to fill with her tears.

Fred loomed up behind with Mr Stone, holding Death's-head, and John Ellis.

"Oh, come in. Come in. Come in."

They trampled snowily into our kitchen.

Frizzy was warmed and wrapped in a blanket with a hot-water bottle and slept at last with Hanna watching beside her. Mum made tea and toast for everybody.

"We can't stay," Fred said. "We've got more to do yet."

"Don't feed the little dog too much at first. Take it easy. As far as we know she's been out on the High Moor in a blizzard and not many live to tell that tale," said Mr Stone.

"Where did you find her?"

"We heard," said one of the others, "that there were some sheep holed up under a snowdrift down Wallabrook way. So we set off and searched around and found a drift shaped by the frost over a rock and a couple of rowan trees in a hollow. Made a proper little cave, out of the wind. And that's where we found the sheep."

"And," said Fred, "when we got them out there was this funny sort of sheep in with 'em."

"But she was always so scared of sheep," cried Tim.

"Reckon they saved her life," said Mr Stone.

"Reckon they did," I said, smiling at my mother.

After they'd gone we sat on beside the fire.

"I'm going to have a baby," Mum said.

Tim's mouth dropped open.

"Why didn't you tell me?" I cried.

"You were so angry with me."

"I'm sorry. But I've not been angry for ages."

"Are you pleased? About the baby?"

"Yep. Great," laughed Tim. "There'll be Frizzy's puppies and a new baby. She doesn't have to go away again, does she?"

"No," smiled Mum. "Of course she can stay. She's come home, hasn't she?"

SUMMERTIME ONCE MORE

Step into our sitting room and you'll see two pictures over the mantelpiece. One is a photograph. It's taken on the moor and shows a clapper bridge over a rock-strewn river. On the bridge stands my aunt Dinah holding hands with Fred who's grinning and on the rocks sits Dad putting a bottle in the water watched by me and Tim. There are three dogs, one red, one white and a hideous black-and-white one. My mother sits on the bank with a carrycot beside her among the remains of a picnic. Asleep on the bank is an old tom cat.

There's a message in the bottle. For Australia, America, Antarctica. Somewhere with an 'A'.

The other picture shows a dog running past a stone wall with the moor behind. She has a red-gold coat and her eyes are bright and mischievous. In the corner is written "*Russet* by Madeleine Sutton".

Widget Sutton
1995

GENE KEMP is the author of many much loved books for children including *The Turbulent Term of Tyke Tiler*, for which she won the Carnegie Medal. She mostly writes school stories but this Goosey Farm story is actually based on real life - when she moved to Devon with her family (her daughter is the Widget in this story). It is a time in Gene's life which she says remains crystal clear: the wild flowers; the birds she'd never seen before; the moors with their bogs and tors, heather and ponies. She would have painted it all if she could. Instead she has written about it.

PAUL HOWARD enjoyed art from an early age and used to draw portraits of his favourite pop stars. On graduating from Leicester Polytechnic, where he studied graphic design, he took a job at the Natural History Museum, refurbishing the dinosaur exhibit amongst other things. He is now a full time artist with three picture books to his credit as well as numerous storybooks.